SNOOP
A Little Help from

Peanuts® characters created
and drawn by Charles M. Schulz

Text by Justine Korman
Backgrounds illustrated by Art and Kim Ellis

A GOLDEN BOOK • NEW YORK
Western Publishing Company, Inc., Racine, Wisconsin 53404

The sun was just coming up when Snoopy awakened
Charlie Brown.

"It's not breakfast time yet," Charlie Brown grumbled.

But Snoopy wasn't asking for his breakfast. He wanted
to say good-bye. He wanted to get an early start on his
camping trip with his friend Woodstock.

"Be careful in the woods," Charlie Brown said, yawning.

Snoopy puffed up his chest. He was an expert camper, had more merit badges than anyone in his Beagle Scout troop, and had won the Puppy Tent Award three years in a row.

Snoopy read off the checklist of equipment to Woodstock.

"Tent. Raft. Sleeping bags. Compass. Map. Fishing tackle. Mess kit."

"I think I forgot something," Snoopy thought. "But what?"

At the park Snoopy soon got bored with the long hiking trail.

"I'll show you how a real camper blazes a trail," he told Woodstock, and he took out his compass and map.

Soon they were up to Snoopy's knees in brambles.

Then they were up to Snoopy's elbows in swamp water. Woodstock rode on Snoopy's hat while the champion Beagle Scout sloshed through the mud.

Woodstock chirped nervously.

"Of course we're not lost," Snoopy said. "Look. There's the trail up ahead. We're probably almost at the campsite by now, thanks to my shortcut."

But when they broke through the bushes onto the trail, Snoopy and Woodstock found themselves...exactly where they had started.

"We can travel much faster by water," declared the world's greatest Beagle Scout. He blew up the rubber raft and set it in the river.

Snoopy was tired from all that hiking and all that
blowing. The gentle water and warm sunshine soon lulled
him to sleep.

Woodstock was the lookout. When he tried to wake
Snoopy, Snoopy rolled over.

"Don't you know you're supposed to let sleeping dogs
lie?" he mumbled.

Finally Woodstock filled his hat with water and poured
it over Snoopy's head.

"Why didn't you wake me before?" Snoopy exclaimed
when he saw what was happening. Their small raft was
headed straight for a waterfall.

"Hang on!" Snoopy yelled as the rushing water carried
them over the falls. He was feeling a little sick.

When they reached the bottom, Snoopy wrung out his Beagle Scout hat. Woodstock emptied the water out of his tiny hiking boots and chirped happily.

"You thought that was fun?" exclaimed Snoopy. "Well, we are *not* going down again!"

Snoopy was tired and hungry. As soon as he and
Woodstock reached the campsite, he took out his mess kit
and told Woodstock to gather wood for a fire.

Soon the campfire was ready.

"Now for the food," Snoopy said. He looked in his backpack. "Oh, no! That's what I forgot!" But Woodstock tapped his tiny backpack. "The food is in there?"

Woodstock nodded. He opened his little backpack and took out his supply.

"One marshmallow?!" Snoopy cried. "You call that food?"

Woodstock chirped an apology. Half a marshmallow was plenty of food for him, he said, but maybe it wasn't the right amount for Snoopy.

"Some camper," Snoopy said angrily. He put the
marshmallow on a stick and started to roast it.
   Woodstock chirped back.
   "I did not get us lost. And I thought you *liked* going
over the falls," Snoopy replied.

As they argued the marshmallow melted and fell
sputtering into the fire. Snoopy and Woodstock looked
from the marshmallow to each other. They were too tired
and hungry to be angry anymore. They started to laugh.

"Everyone makes mistakes," Snoopy said,
"even Beagle Scouts."

Woodstock chirped happily. He was sorry, too.

"We can still get some dinner," Snoopy added.

While Snoopy set up the fishing tackle Woodstock
pulled up worms for bait.

Soon they caught two fish—a big one for Snoopy and a
little one for Woodstock.

Snoopy cooked the fish over the campfire.

After they had eaten, Snoopy and Woodstock sang
songs by the fire.

Then they crawled into their sleeping bags and looked up at the stars.

"Good night," said Snoopy.

Woodstock chirped good night.

But then they both heard noises in the woods—footsteps and snapping twigs. A ghostly light flickered between the trees. The two friends shivered with fear.

It was only good old Charlie Brown, carrying a flashlight.

"Snoopy and Woodstock! Here you are! I was worried, so I came looking for you," Charlie Brown explained. Then he glanced around at the tidy fire and the neat campsite.

"I guess you *are* a great Beagle Scout after all," Charlie
Brown declared.

Snoopy smiled at Woodstock. Snoopy was an expert
camper, all right...with a little help from his friend.